Rumble Doll

copyright 2021 Ron Rundle

all rights reserved

published by Fiesta Creative Arts

printed in United States by Kindle Direct

Publishing

a division of Amazon

ISBN: 9798599752738

to order visit amazon.com

Barnes & Noble or contact me

Text, layout, editing and by

Ron Rundle

ronrundle@gmail.com

https://fiestacreativearts.godaddysites.com

All Titles by R. Rundle

Suggested Grades

Miss Angela (gr. 4 - 6)

The Walker Boys (gr. 4 - 6)

The Dark Side of the Moon (gr. 7 & up)

*Adventures in Babysitting (gr. 5 - 8)

*Adventures in Babysitting: I Have a Dark Passenger (gr. 6 - 8)

Marginal Waters: Monster's Edition (gr. 6 - 8)

This is New (gr. 7 - 10)

Just an Ordinary Joe (gr. 8 - 10)

Pearl (gr. 8 & up)

Rocket Girl (gr. 8 - 10)

There's a New Girl in Town (gr. 7 - 10)

Dragon (gr. 6 - 10)

**The Brat Chronicles (gr. 6 - 8)

**Wherever I Go (gr. 8 & up)

**The Vagabond Gene (gr. 8 & up)

A Passing Ship (gr. 7 & up)

Ride (gr. 8 & up)

**The Vagabond Princess (gr. 8 & up)

High School

Starfinder

High School & Adult

***Marginal Waters

***Marginal Waters: The After Party

***Marginal Waters: The Invasion of the Woodpeckers

***Marginal Waters: I Have a Dark Passenger

***Marginal Waters: The Brat Chronicles

Rumble Doll

Sequential Titles   * ** *

Sundown

Rachel had been stewing about this for as long as she could remember thinking about anything. She had noticed, as soon as she was old enough to notice anything that her family had some missing parts. It contained only her and Gramps, had been that way for as long as she could remember. No mother, father, brother, sister, aunts or uncles, nothing, just her and the old guy sitting to her right on the porch. Also there was never any encouragement to even ask questions and when she did replies were something like,

"Sweetheart, that's a big hard story, maybe when you're older," and that was it. She figured his plan was to brush her off until she just gave up. However, today on the eve of her sixteenth birthday she was like a batter dug in at the plate, with the game riding on this at bat.

"Gramps, what was my mom like?" Always, she thought, a fair point, as she must have had one, unless aliens dropped her from the sky. She got the same, big sigh, and he would take a sip of his beer and look at the floor. This time Rach was going to drive to the hoop.

"Ok, Gramps, give me a time, a date when you're going to tell me. Seventeenth, eighteenth or when I'm old enough to drink?" It was clear that sweetheart number one and only in his life was ticked. He looked at her with complete adoration. He loved her more than he thought was possible, but now she was not an innocent little girl any more. It was time, and she deserved the story.

"Ok darling, but if I got to tell this I need another." Rachel jumped up to get his beer.

"I'll get it, we're losing light." She stopped and turned, "can I have one?" She mimicked what she thought he would say. "No." But to her surprise, he called out.

"Get one for yourself you spoiled little brat." On her way he mumbled to himself,

"You might need it." She was back in a flash and handed him his cold beer.

"It got you two incase the first one gets warm." He took the beer.

"Where'd you hear that?" She shrugged,

"Been cruising the bars for years, and some old guy I know uses it." That gave him a pause, reminding him of the mother in question. He gave her the pointy finger.

"You have not been cruising bars." He took a sip of his beer and looked out across their barnyard at the declining sun. Recalling the past is sometimes, not easy. She took a sip and winced, wondering why the town of High River drank so much of this stuff. It tasted like the sulphur water in the animal trough maybe had a skunk marinating in it for a couple of weeks. He took another sip as Rachel sat staring at him like a cat watching someone eat ice cream. Knowing they were going to get to lick out the bowl if the eater ever got done. He finally got started.

"Rachel, your mom got away from me, somehow." She took another sip and felt it settle in her stomach, starting to figure out what the attraction was. She looked up, more details were required.

"How?" Gramps was still working on how he was going to tell this story. You should know he came from a generation of prairie men who never said, "we need to talk." They kept everything to themselves: old trucks, tools, stories, and especially feelings, but they never talked about them but also never let them go.

"Ok, you got to understand some of my back story as part of this. Came from a strict Baptist background." She took another sip,

"Hot damn, this stuff hits the spot!" He gave her the pointy finger.

"Slow dancing only kiddo." She giggled,

"That's all I do." He gave her a why look, "cause I get to cuddle."

"What am I going to do with you?" She rubbed his shoulder,

"Just love me like you always have." She would say things like that, making him feel like she had given his heart a gentle pat. But it was back to the story she wanted. She was curious.

"Ok what's a Baptist?" He was thinking how to sum it up.

"Ok, lots of work then church for recreation. Church twice on Sunday. Sunday afternoon, read the bible for entertainment, or maybe go crazy and practice the piano.

Then die quietly and hope to hell there's a heaven." Rachel laughed,

"Like here without Sunday." Another pointy finger.

"You take liberties young lady." She giggled,

"Yeah but I'm cute." Then she took another sip and rolled her finger over like the story needed to move on, then burped.

"Oops, ladylike." He just smiled and continued.

"Your mom, didn't take too kindly to the Baptist lifestyle." Rachel thought, duh. Then Gramps looked sad.

"And along came your aunt."

"I had an aunt!" He looked out at the horizon remembering that her eyes were the same cerulean blue as the evening sky. He got reminded of her every day.

"You did, lovely little girl, perfect like you. Her name was Annie. Came home from school one day on the limp, sore knee. We got it checked out, bone cancer." He finished the bottle and started on the other one. "It spread, she had an operation to take off her leg above the knee. Didn't help, more pain, morphine; we were Baptists, so we prayed. The family, the church, the whole town really, and she died anyway. I guess God wasn't fucking listening." He looked at the beer. "I need something stronger if I'm going to continue."

Rachel's eyes widened at the swear word, which he never used. She knew he hadn't got to mom yet. He left and came back with a couple of glasses with some kind of amber liquid in the bottom, and handed one to Rachel. She took a sniff, looked at it and turned up her nose.

"Looks like pee."

"It ain't pee, how am I going to get serious with you joking around?" She pretended to zip her mouth closed.

"Sorry Gramps, go on."

"Your grandmother took it hard, like you would expect. Sat, stared out the window for a couple of years. Drank about twenty gallons of whiskey, then had a stroke and died." Rachel was starting to get why he wasn't interested in talking about this. He had seen other families go through such a loss; it was never good.

"Pretty common for families to blow up after the loss of a child. You know there's no word for that. You can be a widow if you lose a husband. What are you if you lose a child?" Rachel got it.

"No word for it, guess parents don't want to think about it." His eyes saddened again,

"They do not. Your mother at that point, I think, just snapped. I guess it was all too much; maybe she thought she was next, but I don't know for sure. She quit school, took a job in town, became a bit of a party girl. She got real popular with the boys in town, if you get my drift." Rachel got it, there were a few girls in her school like that. Rachel asked,

"Then what?" He took his drink and downed the whole shot in one go.

"Come on. bring yours, I might need it." He got up with a grunt like he always did, then wobbled. The beer and whiskey was starting to kick it. Rachel got closer to him.

"Put your hand on my shoulder old guy." He did and just smiled. She was such a sweetheart.

"Come on." They headed for the barn, not exactly as the crow flies. Gramps needed his course corrected a few times. Rachel wondered how many times she had crossed the barnyard for chores. They finally headed for an attached shed, no windows and double doors, always locked. It like other issues in the family were never opened, until now. Gramps fiddled with the lock, opened the doors and turned on a single overhead light. There was nothing inside but gloom and a large lump under a tarp. He took Rachel's drink and drank it in one gulp. What was under the tarp was obviously another issue. He pulled it off and underneath was a light green coloured car, convertible, with the top down, rounded lines. Rachel was impressed,

"Spiffy car!" Gramps ran his hand along its curved fenders.

"She's a peach, your great grandfather gave it to your mother before he died." Rachel was checking it out, thinking how cool she would look at the wheel.

"What is it?"

"It's a 1938 Chevy convertible." They stopped at the back and Rachel noticed,

"No trunk." There was just a seat where the trunk should be. Gramps noted,

"That's called a Rumble Seat; the English call it a Dickey." Rachel just looked inside, wondering, so? "Your mom apparently used to entertain there." He put a little emphasis on entertain. "Her nickname was Rumble Doll." Rachel indeed got it, sex doesn't remain a mystery to farm girls for long. Most animals are hard at it whenever they can.

She remembered her first sex education lesson. A rooster was chasing a chicken around the barnyard and finally jumped on her back. Rachel asked,

"What's he doing?" Gramps with succinct prairie brevity said,

"Making more chickens." Rachel asked,

"So people do it..." Before she could finish the sentence he just said,

"Yep," Clarity came on the next demonstration she observed. This one was significantly more graphic. Mung their old bull was doing the same thing to a cow. At that point she was really glad she wasn't born a cow.

Back to the present, she looked down into the seat. She had to admit to herself she was picturing the various ergonomic possibilities in such a small space. Young girls think about sex but most enter the activity with some reservation. Rachel figured out her origin.

"So I was conceived in the rumble seat of a 38 Chevy?" Gramps nodded.

"Could have been the front seat, I wasn't there." Rachel got it, thinking, but did not say, a little more room to manoeuvre especially with the top down. However there was the possibility of the gear lever getting in the way. She winced, thinking, wouldn't want to sit on that. She asked,

"Can I get behind the wheel?" Gramps laughed,

"Sure don't think too much went on there." Rachel opened the door and looked for residue, just in case. If there was evidence it had been removed so she slid into the driver's seat, noting the stick shift falling to hand, no problem. She had been driving tractors and Gramp's pickup truck around the farm for years.

"This is kind of nice." Gramps leaned on the door frame.

"Don't think she really drove it much." Rachel added,

"Guess it was parked a lot." Gramps nodded.

"I heard stories, you want the car?" Rachel thought for about a tenth of a second.

"Heck yeah!" She pictured her self driving to school with top down, hat and sunglasses on. Figured she'd very much pass on her mother's none driving use.

"Come on back to the house there's more." Rachel figured, got to be, haven't rounded up where the heck is good old mom yet.

Back up on the porch Gramps went in and got two more shots and handed one to Rachel.

"This is just for tonight, young lady." Rachel giggled,

"Got any cigars?" He just gave her a look and got serious.

"Ok, well your mother's activities got her pregnant, obviously, with you. Came home one day and told me. I asked, 'what you going to do?' All I got was a shrug, got a lot of that from her as a teenager. She sat around home and waited too long to do anything about it. I figured all that was her call anyway, and, I'm really glad she didn't." Rachel smiled up at him.

"You wouldn't have me." Another adoring look,

"I would not indeed."

He took a sip, knowing the next part was going to be the hardest. "She sat around and got bigger until she had you. I didn't even know when she went to the hospital, didn't know when she was coming home, got nothing. The day she came home I was sitting by the pond on the big rock we used to tether the old bull. Figured I could chain myself to the rock and roll it in the pond, end it all. But, I figured, who would feed and water the animals, couldn't do that. Came close though, I was right at the bottom of the well then. Came back to the house and there you were, all wrapped up, asleep, lots of black hair, so cute." He drank half the whiskey in his glass. "She was gone, she just left you, haven't seen or heard from her since. If I had done the pond thing, you would have died, no one could hear you crying out here. Can't think of anything more horrible than that. And here you are, smart, beautiful and such a sweetheart, so glad you're here. Best thing I never did in my life." With that Rachel jumped up and wrapped her arms around him.

"And you looked after me by yourself."

"My absolute pleasure darling." She took the glass and drank her whiskey in one gulp, and grabbed her throat.

"Gramps, no offence, but that's like drinking fire!" She sat down and saw Gramps looking off over the field, never saw him look sadder. He turned and looked at her with tears in his eyes that she had never seen before.

"I lost them all Rach, couldn't help Annie, prayed, we all did, didn't help at all. Didn't know what to say to your grandmother, couldn't help her either. And your mom, I never had any idea what she was thinking, ever. I knew she wasn't happy, but I don't know how she could have left you. I just lost them all." Rachel gave him another hug,

"You didn't lose me." He stood up and gave her a kiss on top of the head.

"No, I didn't, but let's hit the hay, that's enough stories for today." Rachel agreed,

"It sure is."

Marie Bartlet

Marie sat on the balcony of her suite overlooking Almeria harbour. It was as far away from High River as she could get. It was not so much in distance, but in weather and circumstance. Before she had migrated to this location in Spain she researched it and found it had never had a recorded temperature below freezing. This was a selling feature as Marie found you froze your ass off from October to May in High River. Also, it was a popular tourist town with a large safe harbour for transient boats. Lots of bars and restaurants, many were on the high end. The attraction was the harbour with lots of large boats coming and going. She discovered they didn't run on loose change so the captains had to be well heeled.

Her relocation from High River to Almeria had been caused in her opinion by a slowly festering hatred for everything her family and community stood for. Life was a continuous Baptist bible study, every meal starting off with a long litany of thanks for food that had been produced by hard working farmers, and prepared by hard working wives, not

God. Dinner conversations was a continuation of Grace. At one point she remembered blowing up and yelled,

"Can we just fucking eat!"

Sundays were extra special, church twice, in the afternoon you could read the bible or practice the piano for entertainment. And church, in her mind was where clocks stood still as it seemed like the longest recorded hour in the history of time. The communion litany was extra special.

"We are not worthy to even gather up the crumbs from under Your Table." She thought on more than one occasion, keep the fucking crumbs. She came to the conclusion that life could be summed up as follows: give constant thanks for the opportunity to work like a rented mule, have no fun at all, then die. Supposedly your reward for being such a good soldier will be in heaven.

Then along came the cruelest of tragedies, her young sister Annie. She was the sweetest of sweethearts and got cancer. Why, well the local knowledge was that it was God's will or plan. That plan or the reason for it appeared to be unavailable to the people affected by it. It sounded so stupid she couldn't even bring herself to think about it. The treatment seemed to be more painful than the disease. Of course, everybody prayed; she even tried, and it took about six months for this lovely little girl to shrink to living skeleton. She would scream if anyone tried to move her. Marie was told that her suffering made us all stronger and that Annie would soon be in a better place, most likely riding horses with Jesus. During the service there was lots of talk about the kingdom of heaven and salvation. Various people started shouting out what was for sure in their view, life affirming.

"Praise the Lord, for our salvation!"

"Jesus we love you!"

"Thank you God for our faith?"

It was at that point that Marie snapped.

"Shut the fuck up you morons; there's a little girl in that box, dead. Not going to be riding horses with Jesus!" She stormed out of the service, never to return. From a distance during the burial she stood and watched her sister being lowered into the ground. That's a picture she knew she would never forget.

Her mom coped by going in the whiskey bottle. Marie saw first hand what happens to a woman that loses a child. Marie, and everything else was forgotten in her mother's grief. At fifteen she came to a conclusion from many observations that the whole Baptist thing was just bullshit based on the sale of an invisible product.

She had a year long experiment as the Rumble Doll of High River. However she did not find getting defiled by hillbillies very rewarding either, along with some painful hangovers. She remembers waking up one summer morning in the back of her car. Couldn't remember how she got there but since she had no underwear on figured there was a boy involved. He was long gone, left her with a hangover and no panties. The local hillbillies often took them as some kind of trophy. She then realized she needed some kind of plan. Preferably one with an escape clause that did not include losing your underwear.

She managed to escape to Europe with a little money and the genetic make up to survive. You might ask how can you survive in a foreign country with only a high school education and no real marketable skills? The only Spanish she knew was,

"Chica Caliente." It means hot girl; it was on a 'T' shirt she bought.

Well you somehow sell what you have and Marie was a very attractive young woman. She was smart, fit and a pretty good actress for the theatre she was soon to star in.

Her modus operandi was find a high end hotel lounge and sit reading her Kindle. Soon the bar tender would arrive and whisper.

"The man at that table wants to know what you like to drink." She had a favourite.

"Chateau Cheval Blanc 2014" Now it wasn't so rare or expensive that high end bars wouldn't have it, but it wasn't cheap either at $500 a bottle. This weeded out the suitors that couldn't keep her in a way that she required. Soon a glass would arrive and she sniffed it; she knew its aroma. If it was genuine she would take a sip, if not, simply push it away. If she took a sip, soon the gentleman would arrive.

"May I sit?" Now when a guy spends $500 on a drink the least you can do is talk to him, and it went from there. As she sat she was recalling her past as a very young transplant to Spain. The question was, how can a young girl somehow live off the land so to speak, without being a hooker? Before she figured out the bar con she was walking along the harbour and saw a sign on a sailboat,

'Deckhand quería' She stopped and took out her English to Spanish dictionary. She knew what deckhand was and figured out what queía meant. She stood looking at the boat until a guy appeared. She smiled,

"You need a deckhand?" He was an older guy and looked her over and nodded.

"Tienes experiencia?" Back to the dictionary, but sort of figured it out. She gave him her innocent girl smile and shook her head.

"No." She was just seventeen at the time, but not even close to innocent when it came to dealing with men. She was wearing a red 'T' shirt that was too short and too tight with no bra, and cut off slightly shredded blue jeans that were too short top and bottom. Of course this was a guy and an older one at that. After looking at her credentials, he didn't care if she knew what a boat was and motioned for her to come aboard.

They went from there, and she was hired for the summer. He had money and paid her $300 U.S. a day. Along with that he taught her Spanish. She was charming, fit and handy around the boat, but mainly charming and decorative. In the afternoon when there was nothing to do she would lounge on a deck pad in her bikini while he sat at the tiller in admiration. They got to know each other well and got along well. There was no sexual component though he certainly thought about it but when he knew she was seventeen he couldn't as she was younger than his daughter. And he knew the age of consent was sixteen in Spain, but looking at her, you could guess wrong.

She managed to accumulate about eighteen thousand U.S. dollars by the end of the summer and became a sought after deckhand in her first boss's yacht club. She leaned how to sail, learned Spanish, stayed fit, and could charm the last ten dollars off a starving man if she had to. In going from port to port she got lots of attention from most anybody male who would ask her out but she would say.

"No gracias estoy con…" Basically, no thank you I'm with, whoever was paying her to be a deckhand. She discovered that loyalty is appreciated. And truthfully she'd had more than enough casual sex in her young life. Since room and board was provided by the boat owner, all the money she made was banked. Being a cute and charming deckhand was a lot more lucrative than waiting tables at High River. She did that through her teen years and then graduated to the 'confidant' level in her twenties. Her years of putting out in the rumble seat of her car for a six pack of beer, and the joy of having your underwear stolen were gone.

She got very good at gauging her suitors. Most were extremely shy at even suggesting she sleep with them, and often gave her gifts and raises without strings, just hoping she would consider them. She found older men were the most appreciative, gentlemanly and were also well funded. Rarely someone would assume because most of her butt was visible in her bikini you could give it a pat. She would just shake her head no and if it happened again, she was gone at the next port.

Red Maserati

Back in High River things were looking pretty good for Rachel. She got to take her new car to school rather than ride the noisy school bus. She was heading home from school one fine spring day, top down, all was right with the world. She noticed a shiny red convertible pulled over. Also a fairly good looking guy was walking to the front of the car.

Now out west people aren't left stranded beside the road. It was not a deserted highway so she was ok, not that her Gramps would have that opinion. But she was curious and pulled over. He had the hood up and was looking at the engine bay as she walking up and noticed, Maserati, from Ontario, ok, not a local hillbilly.

"Got trouble there?" He looked up and smiled.

"Check coolant light came on, just a little low." Rachel to the rescue.

"I got some." She headed for her car and fished a jug out of the rumble seat, now used for storage not entertainment. "There you go, nice car by the way." He topped it up, giving her a chance to check out his butt which was ok too. He gave it back to her noticing her car.

"Hey nice car too." He headed for hers. "Way cool how old is it. They stopped and looked inside.

"1938 Chevy convertible. It was my mom's." She leaned closer to him and whispered, it's called Rumble Doll."

"Cool name for a car, got to be a story."

"Well word is she used to entertain in the rumble seat." He pointed,

"Back there?" They were looking down into the seat she knew he was thinking the same thing, not much room. To change the mood she asked,

"Where you headed?" He shrugged,

"Just on a road trip. Can I sit in your car?" She even opened the door.

"Sure hop in, I cleaned out the old condoms." He did take a look and got in, grabbing the wheel.

"Way cool a stick shift, you're a girl that can handle a stick." At that point Rachel thought of something extremely rude to say but managed to keep a sock in it and asked,

"Ok what's your name stranger?" He gave her a smile she liked.

"Mike Sargent, yours?" She held out her hand.

"Rachel." He shook it.

"No last name." She leaned closer. "I can't tell you I'm under cover." He laughed,

"As what?" And before the filter worked it came out.

"Nothing, I just like it under the covers." She realized and put her hands over her face, when she took them away her face was red.

"Sorry, I say things sometimes, my mother's genes maybe." He looked at her amused.

"You're funny and really cute. Oh by the way, you know of any farms that need a some extra help, I'm handy." Rachel used a line she'd heard before.

"If girls don't find you hansom, at least let then find you handy." He gave her an amused look; he was discovering she was a bit of a pistol.

"So any farms need work."

"Well Mike this is your lucky day, we do, follow me home, we'll take a meeting. Before we go can I sit in your way cool car. She got in and looked around running her hand over the leather seat.

"Smooth as a ducks bum." She put her hands on the wheel, "paddle shifts, looks like fun." Mike said,

"Your want to drive it home, I'll follow in yours?" Rachel didn't think long.

"Heck yeah," and flipped him the keys to Rumble Doll. She started the car and blipped the throttle a couple of times.

"Ok then." Mike put his hand on the wheel.

"Remember, you got 600hp there." She gave him a slightly evil grin.

"Ok then," and took off. He yelled after her.

"600 horse power!" He ran for her car afraid she would lose him in the first turn.

In a few minutes Rachel roared into their farmyard and skidded to a halt. Gramps was sitting on their porch, feet up, sipping a beer.

"Hi Gramps, traded her even for Rumble Doll." He smiled, knew there was more to the story.

"Ok, good deal." Just then Mike came in with Rachel's car and rolled to a gentle stop. He got out and came over;

Rachel was still in his car, at least looking sheepish. He was twirling her keys on his finger.

"Have fun?" She giggled,

"Sorry, but I'm cute." Gramps intervened.

"I see you've met Rachel, come on up son and have a general sit, you look like a man who could use a beer." They both came up and Rachel did the honours.

"Gramps this is Mike Sargent, he's looking for farm hand work. We need some help, right?" Gramps handed Mike a beer and shook his hand. Gramps did glance at the red Maserati and wondered why you would need to find work if you could afford that car.

"Ok son if you are going to hang around I need your back story." Also, though not stated, if you're going to hang around my granddaughter. He looked and noticed the plates. "You're a long way from home."

"Yes sir, just finished two years of medical school, had a visit at a children's cancer clinic." He took a moment. "Don't know if I can do it." Gramps nodded, remembering poor Annie. "My dad was cool said, 'take a road trip, clear your head. You don't want to be unhappy for the rest of your life.' So, here I am; where am I again?" Gramps smiled,

"High River Alberta, Bartlet Farm." Rachel had gone inside and came out.

"Gosh had to get my own beer, come on guys, shift your carcasses over let the girl have a spot." She pushed her chair between them. "Look at that a prairie flower between two cactus." Gramps gave her a look.

"You'll find that Rachel takes liberties." He thought for a minute. "Ok Mike, I can pay $100 a day with room and board. You can stay in the bunkie over there and eat with us. We milk at seven in the morning and six at night." Rachel gave a silent fist pump; she liked Mike right off and wanted him to hang around. Mike said,

"I can set up the milking equipment for the milk, done it before. And I can cook, like it, I'll make dinner. Rachel blurted out,

"How 'bout we get married tomorrow. I'll skip school, put Gramps in a home." They all laughed at that. Gramps got up and wrapped his arms around Rachel.

"You little…you do take liberties." Then kissed her on top of the head." They all settled back and had a beer before bed. It was a good day at the Bartlet farm.

Marcus Rossi

Enter Marcus Rossi to the story. He was one of several confidants that Marie travelled with after she graduated from deckhand. Although she was more deck decoration than deckhand. How did Marcus Rossi of Barcelona Spain end up with Marie Bartlet, the Rumble Doll of High River Alberta? It was a combination of chance, circumstance and precision planning.

His own back story was very different from Marie's. He was born into money; his dad owned a few car dealerships, a private investigation firm and a large construction company. Young Marcus figured he'd just wait around until he was of working age and take over one of his father's businesses. He'd take over them all when his dad retired. The plan was to find one where minimal work was required. As a result of this attitude his progress at a very expensive private school was minimal. His father got tired of receiving phone calls regarding his under achieving son to the point where the hammer came down.

Marcus was called into his home office. Now he figured it wasn't serious because other than not working much Marcus had never really done anything bad. His dad was unusually curt.

"Sit son." He let him stew a bit while he pretended to be reading a report. He finally looked up. "It has come to my attention you are just wasting your time, the school's time and my money." Marcus just shrugged, not the response his dad was looking for.

"Ok, since you're sixteen you are quitting school and going to work." Marcus was still not concerned figuring he could get a nice clean, cushy desk job at one of his dad's businesses.

"Ok father." At least this time a little more respectful. Father had a plan.

"You are working for Rossi Construction, in the yard, general labour." Not what young Marcus wanted to hear. He had visited his dad's construction sites when he was little but didn't figure he'd actually end up pushing wheelbarrows full of cement around. His dad continued,

"If you start in the office the men will have no respect for you and you will never learn what it's like to work." Marcus tried to resist,

"But, Dad..." Before he could complete the sentence his dad said,

"You start on Monday at seven a.m." He handed him a card with the address on it. "Better get yourself some safety shoes." Marcus tried his last tactic.

"What's mom think about this?" His dad smiled, Marcus was her one and only son, and generally gave him more leeway.

"Well you can try but your mother and I have discussed this, we are in agreement."

So Marcus learned how to work. He dumped a few loads of cement pushing wheelbarrows along planks, much to the laugher of his yard mates. But he learned to laugh with them and slowly grew up, got fitter and stronger. He learned that real men get up and to work on time, do their job and pay their bills. He gradually got experience in all aspects of his dad's business. When he was thirty his father said,

"Son I am retiring to various trout streams around the world. Rossi Enterprises is yours, you have become a man and I am very proud of you and trust you completely to manage the family businesses."

From there Marcus made only one mistake; it was of a personal nature. He married within his snack bracket. It was almost an arranged marriage, but she beautiful and charming. Unfortunately she was an indolent young woman who did not have parents who insisted she learn how to work at something. Her life was basically getting ready for lunch and shopping. Children were of no interest either as having one looked like a lot more work than she wanted. Also they had to be looked after for who knows how long. She was a hot house orchid and her husband was a worker and loved outdoor recreational activities. So with nothing at all in common, her and Marcus slowly drifted apart. A divorce was too expensive so he just funded her lifestyle and continued on his own. Mostly he continued with work, making more money than even he or his wife could spend and taking very little time for vacations.

However one day on a much needed week's vacation he ran his boat from Barcelona to Almeria. It was a beautiful day and turning into a warm summer evening on the Mediterranean. Luck would have it on the same evening Marie was sitting at a dockside cafe at Almeria. It had been a quiet evening, as she even had to buy her own drink and was wondering if she had lost her touch. She was amusing herself by watching a fairly large boat slowly coming into a nearby slip. The captain manoeuvred it skillfully and got off tying up the boat himself. Marie thought, good, no deckhands or bow bunnies. The guy looked pretty good and obviously had money.

With his boat tied up and plugged into shore power Marcus poured himself a drink and sat on his back deck for an evening of girl watching and hoped for a little luck in the pleasures of the harbour department. Little did he know he was being scouted by an experienced, and one even might say a professional flirt. Because of her significant resources she was playing a game only she could win.

She noticed a harbour light just a few meters from his boat. Now she was wearing one of her subtle yet effective 'come and get me dresses' from her collection. It was very thin material, light cream in colour. Now in the shadows it just looked like a nice summer dress, but backlit it highlighted the very trim, shapely, and slightly tanned woman inside it. She wandered slowly down the dock and brushed her hand over the toe rail of his boat very near where Marcus was sitting and just said,

"Bonito barco," and kept on walking. Marcus looked up and saw what he was supposed to see. He had to ask,

"¿Quieres una bebida miss" She stopped and did the model turn she had learned. It's where you pivot both feet at the same time so the dress you are wearing flares out. You also keep your feet close together to accentuate the hips. He saw the rest and that was that. Then she smiled,

"I would love one."

Marcus and Marie stayed together for almost a year. Her well orchestrated flirtation had turned into a long term relationship with Marcus. She knew he worshipped the ground she walked on enough to keep her in the current expensive digs overlooking the Almeria harbour. It was a place for them to meet when he could get away from work. She was comfortable on her own, walked, kept fit and read in the shade of her balcony. She had graduated from deckhand to confidant and life was very good.

It was also good for Marcus; she was either smart enough to just do what he liked or genuinely enthusiastic about his recreational activities. He liked boating in the summer and skiing in the Alps in the winter. She was young and more than fit enough to participate in all his interests. She kept herself informed and was always an interesting and amusing dinner companion. In the bedroom she did everything a woman can do, and let a man do everything he could do as long as there was no pain. As an added bonus she had learned shiatsu and massage. When Marcus came to her suite after a long day she never said much, just pored him a drink and took off his jacket and shirt and started working on his shoulders. If he'd had a day at his construction sites and was on his feet should would massage them as well. He would often feel guilty about the attention.

"Marie, you don't have to…" She would shhh him and say.

"I've been sitting by the pool reading, let me." As a result this and the rest, he fell in love with her completely even though in many ways he didn't really understand her. It's a question that has been asked, can you love completely without complete understanding? For him the answer was yes.

They were sitting one evening after dinner and before bed time. She had her favourite wine and he his single malt Scotch. She asked a surprise question, almost seemed like business.

"Marcus how hard is it to find someone?"

"Depends where. who are you looking for?" She was looking unsure for the first time in their relationship, mainly because he knew none of her backstory. She didn't figure on sharing the fact that she had worked herself through the senior boys football team in her senior year at high school. She was worried he would be judgmental to the point of moving on. She summed it up concisely, with a lot of information management.

"My past contained some unfortunate choices." He was now curious.

"How so?" She decided to tell him and went through the highlights, omitting the Rumble Doll details and the fact that she left her baby on the couch and took off. She just said she was ill equipped to raise a child at sixteen and it was left for adoption. Again, true but not exactly the whole story. Even so he easily connected the details.

"You want to see if your daughter and dad are ok." Marie actually had a few tears,

"It's her sixteenth birthday tomorrow; I just want to know if they're ok."

"You know where they are" She sniffed,

"High River, Alberta Canada, can't see them moving." He would do anything for her.

"I'll send one of my men." Like she often did, came over and climbed in his lap and kissed him.

"What would I do without you? That of course was a question with many possible answers. However Marcus followed one of Walt Whitman's rules of ethics.

"Be curious, not judgemental."

Rachel and the Red Maserati

Mike proved to be an outstanding farm hand, knowledgeable about dairy farming and hard working. He and Rachel were also getting along as Mother Nature continued her relentless work. Gramps saw and knew it was bound to happen at some point. It did remind him that some day she would likely move away and a boy would be at the bottom of it. He really didn't want to think too much about that possibility.

One afternoon Gramps was on an errand as the kids patrolled the fence line in an ATV and had stopped for lunch. Rachel and her Gramps always stopped at this spot. It had good shade beside a spring feed creek that ran through their property. It was a typical Alberta mid summer day; Mike noted.

"A little warm." Rachel was an old hand at this.

"Let's take a dip in the creek; it's refreshing."

"In what?" Rachel figured.

"You got underwear under the jeans." Mike thought,

"I don't think so", not knowing Rachel. She peeled off her 'T' shirt and cut off jeans in a flash and headed for the water.

"Chick, chick, chicken." Mike called to her.

"I'll be the life guard." Part way down she stopped and turned.

"You staring at my butt?" He smiled.

"I'll say this, you look good going away."

"So how is it, I don't see it?" He laughed,

"You could crack an egg on that butt." She laughed and headed for the water, splashing around.

"Bit nippy." Mike had to be honest, he was looking forward to her coming out. In about two minutes his wish was granted. She came out heading for the sunshine. Now her underwear was not heavy duty as she really didn't need much support and now wet. Let's say it didn't leave much to the imagination. Also, she was a fit sixteen and right at the top of her game. Part way back she stopped and looked down.

"Oops!" And covered what her hands would. "Got my high beams on." Mike couldn't believe she just said that, as she stopped in front of him.

"Could you get a towel out of the shore box please." He got it and looked away handing it to her. For some reason she was apologetic.

"Sorry."

"Sorry, that was the highlight of my summer!" She blushed a little hustled to dry herself off and get her shorts and 'T' shirt on.

"There, decent now." She ran her hands through her hair, "bit of a tangle." Mike asked,

"You got a comb?" She dug into the shore box.

"Yep." Mike offered.

"I'll comb out your hair if you want." She blushed slightly and sat down with her back to him.

"You bet." He actually just wanted to touch her somehow. Mother Nature was sitting in a nearby tree, relaxing and thought, this game is easy, just a matter of time. Mike gently combed out her long auburn hair until it lay neatly on her back. She hadn't had that done since she was a little girl, and decided it was very nice.

Meanwhile on a hill overlooking where the kids were Marcus's investigator was taking some pictures, mainly of

Rachel to send back to his boss. Gramps was heading home and spotted the man with a camera and he was obviously taking pictures of his beloved granddaughter. He got out of his truck in some annoyance.

"What the hell you doing?" The guys was startled.

"Just taking some landscape shots of the property. Gramps looked down and figured that was not what he was doing.

"Get the hell out of here! And give me that camera!" Now two things, one the pics had already been sent via email and the man was not giving up his camera.

"I'll leave, calm down, not doing anything." At that point Gramps slumped against the guardrail. "You ok sir?" It was obvious that he was not ok. The guy just wanted to get out of there and called 911 and was gone.

Rachel was sitting looking dreamy when Mike looked up.

"There's flashing lights on the hill.

"That's near our property, let's check it out." The ride up the hill didn't take long, when they got there the ambulance driver was just closing the door. He knew Rachel.

"Rach, your Gramps is in back, follow me to the hospital." Mike said,

"Go, I'll head back on foot, do the chores." The ambulance was faster than Rachel's ATV and when she got there the doctor met her at the emergency room door. Rachel knew before he talked to her.

The next few days were just a blur for her, the viewing, service, burial and reception were just hazy recollections. Mike just did the chores, thinking a couple of times about how much easier it was on the road, but couldn't leave her, not now. Rachel spent most of a week just sitting on the porch looking at nothing. Every once in awhile she would start crying and Mike knew there was not much he could do or say, other than do the chores. He did take a few glances at his dad's Maserati, parked under a tree, waiting. The carefree highway was calling.

The Prodigal Daughter?

A short time later Marie was sitting on the balcony of her suite. Marcus had said the information she wanted was available and his investigator was on his way. He had a feeling this would open a can of worms.

"You sure you want all this?" She nodded, taking a few sips of her wine. It currently wasn't helping much.

"I do, you know anything?" Marcus shook his head.

"His plane hasn't been on the ground more than an hour.

Before she was ready the agent was sitting with them overlooking the harbour, his laptop on a table in front of her.

"Miss I have pictures of what I believe is your daughter and it looks like a boyfriend or farmhand, don't know for sure." She just motioned for him to turn his laptop around. She sat and scrolled though the pictures. A young girl splashing in the creeks she had skinny dipped in herself. Also sitting and getting her hair combed out. She was thinking, that ain't no farmhand. Marcus asked,

"May I?" She just pushed the laptop his way, and looked out at the harbour. He scanned through the pictures and looked at her, waiting for her to say what he knew. She turned back when she knew he was finished.

"She's me! Identical!" Marcus nodded.

"Never saw a kid look more like her mother, she's your girl alright." The agent said,

"There's one more thing. An older man saw me taking pictures, got really upset and had some kind of episode. I called 911 and left when I heard the ambulance, so I don't know, how he is. Marie just turned and faced the harbour again and picked up her wine. Marcus handed the agent an envelope and nodded for him to go. He sat wondering what to say and decided to just wait, see what she would do. He knew what he would be doing whatever she wanted, but truly had no idea what her response would be. She finally turned to him.

"I want to go and see them." He actually smiled.

"Yes, I would if I were you."

"She could be my sister." He nodded in agreement.

"Yes, she's beautiful, just like her mother." Marie grabbed her phone.

"I'll book a flight from Barcelona, should be interesting how to get to High River. Marcus was thinking.

"Do they have an airport?" Marie rolled her eyes, recalling making out in her car with a bottle of wine and some hillbilly wishing a plane would come over to break the monotony of being defiled by Jimmy, Billy-Bob, whatever.

"Yes they have an airport." He moved closer to her.

"Take my jet, he'll take you right there."

"Marcus no, too expensive." He motioned for her to come and sit in his lap; he knew that was a mistake. At close range she was almost like a drug he had to have.

"I insist, I have money, you can leave tomorrow." She tapped him on the nose with her pointer finger.

"How much is that going to cost?"

"Not your concern." She hugged him, having a knack of enveloping his face in her hair and breasts at the same time.

Soon she looked down and saw Barcelona disappearing under the wings of Marcus's wide body executive jet. She was the only passenger other than the pilot and a charming stewardess who was there to get her anything she needed or wanted. When they levelled out she came by.

"Ok to unbuckle miss, Marcus left a few bottles of your favourite wine, want some?" Marie actually smiled.

"Oh I think so, thank you." From there she sipped wine, listened to music and napped. She decided air travel was turning her into a cat. She blushed thinking I've carved out a good life with Petunia down there. It was her nickname for some would say her well used body part. She soon was stirred gently by her stewardess.

"Miss we're on approach; buckle up well, the runway is short." This did cause some alarm.

"I'm not going to die am I?" The young woman smiled.

"No, but the pilot will be hard on the brakes." She looked out the window and saw the ground coming up at an alarming rate, then the screech of tires on the runway. She was right, he was hard on the brakes but she soon heard the plane's engines spooling down as he taxied gently towards the airport terminal.

Soon she found herself standing alone on the runway with her luggage. The airport terminal was closed; more of a portable building than a terminal. Not exactly Le Guardia where they stopped for fuel. The familiar blast of Alberta summer reflected on the tarmac was welcoming her home.

"Well now what, is there a taxi in this hick town by now." A voice startled her.

"I can take you where you want to go miss." The voice was the usual High River hillbilly but he looked friendly. She was familiar with the species. This one was sitting on a golf cart towing a small trailer. It was not exactly Marcus's chauffeur driven limousine. She at least smiled.

Hight River Motel?"

"Hop on miss, I know where it is." He was already starting to load her luggage on the trailer. She figured it was this or walk through town towing her belongings, and she did not travel light. However, on went the hat and sunglasses, didn't want some former fan to spot her riding through town. She thought, or maybe make a grand entrance and strip naked, ride through town like Lady Godiva. Her friendly driver of course wanted to talk.

"What brings you to town?"

"Just visiting an old confidant." This gave the driver something to think about because she was certain he didn't know what a confidant was. He got quiet so it appeared to be working. The town looked pretty much the same as she was driven though, and in no time.

"We're here." Marie wanted to make sure.

"Could you just wait until I see it they have my reservation?" Again, friendly,

"You bet miss." The inside of the motel was pretty much early Canadian economy, not exactly her Almeria suit. An older woman appeared and not very welcoming even though it appeared she didn't have too many customers.

"Help you?"

"I have a reservation, Rossi." She slid the platinum Master Card across the counter. The woman looked at it.

"Don't get too many of these." Marie who had to admit to herself, she was a little bitchy and looked around the place and said,

"No, I guess not." The subtle put down was noticed by the proprietor. She looked Marie up and down and said,

"No visitors." Marie stiffened at what she was sure was not a subtle accusation.

"Give me my card back." The woman looked and did. "I am not a fucking hooker!" Marie did the model turn and left, thinking, ok, plan 'B'. Her friendly driver already had her bags off the golf cart.

"Which room?" Marie thought.

"Change of plan, I think the owner has fleas." He was taken aback.

"Ok."

"Do you know of any cottages in the area?" The driver appeared excited.

"Miss you are in luck, my brother and I own one, just on the edge of town, restaurant next door, cold beer and the food won't kill you right away." Marie smiled at the ringing endorsement. She had to admit, he was a little funny.

"Sounds good, how much for a month?" She thought she might as well be generous with Marcus's money even though a month was not going to happen.

"How about $800?" Marie peeled off ten $100 bills.

"There." He looked, actually counting as she went.

"Miss, that's too much." Marie would have none of it.

"No, take it, you were kind to me."

And so evening found her sitting on the small back deck of the cottage overlooking the actual High River sipping her favourite wine. She could see a half a dozen of her make out spots from her current location. She had liberated the two bottles Marcus had left for her on the jet. No point sending them back home.

For the next few days she found herself as somewhat of a voyeur tourist, visiting various places she used to entertain, marvelling at recalling how much of an absolute slut she was. But most of her time was spent parked on a hill overlooking her old family farm. She was hoping to see her Rachel. She had finally found out her name from the researcher, but if she was still on the farm she hadn't seen her just what was either her live in boyfriend or a farmhand.

She was starting to wonder then got a clue in a text from Marcus, saying his researcher had done more digging and had to inform that her dad had indeed died from an apparent heart attack. When she read it, she had to sit down, she knew her daughter was now an orphan, well de-facto orphan. This however, did not bring the mother of the year out of hiding to perhaps comfort her only child. She did wonder how she would be doing with all this and knew it would be difficult to run the farm on her own.

Then for some reason she started to cry and this was new, she couldn't even remember the last time she cried. What was it, concern, guilt, was her suppressed conscience coming to the surface? She called her confidant who it just now occurred to her was her only friend in the world. When he answered he knew something was wrong.

"Marcus."

"Are you crying? Are you hurt?" She sniffed,

"Not hurt, just upset; I don't know, just read your text about my dad."

"I know, sorry, couldn't think of any good way to tell you thought you should know."

"My daughter is an orphan."

"What do you want to do?" Then came what he really did not expect.

"I think I should try to see her, in person." Marcus said immediately.

"I'll come, you shouldn't do that alone." With that she really burst into tears, but recovered after a bit.

"I love you, you know." He said the right words and he did indeed love her.

"I'll be there tomorrow." She was starting to feel better; he definitely was the guy to have on your side.

"Text me when you're getting close; I have a car, I'll pick you up."

Back at the Bartlet Homestead

Rachel had spent the last few days sitting on her deck just looking out at the fields. She drank beer in the evening until it put her to sleep. Mike was being everything, farm labour, chief cook and bottle washer. And in the down time he just sat with her and said nothing. What can you say to a girl who lost her whole family and was now facing farm chores alone. As the week went on Mike wondered how long he could do this without going nuts himself.

He got his answer, about ten o'clock one night there was a knock on his bunkie room door. When he opened it, it was Rachel in her p.j.s holding her pillow.

"Hi Mike, I can't cry anymore, but I don't want to be alone. Thanks so much for doing the chores; I'm back to work tomorrow. But tonight, I want you to make me forget, for a couple of hours anyway."

"You sure?" She held it up.

"I brought my own pillow." He just said,

"Come here."

Morning came and Rachel woke up to the smell of bacon and eggs. Her lover was also her chef. She wandered into the kitchen and caught a glimpse of herself in the mirror.

"I look like an unmade bed." Mike laughed,

"I think that was the general idea, did it work?" She forgot.

"What?"

"Did you forget for a couple of hours." She smiled and came over and gave him a kiss.

"I did."

"Next, are you hungry?" She had been living on beer for a few days and now was feeling much better.

"Fuck yeah!"

After that Mike moved into the main house with her, and Rachel got back into the swing of things. She was hoping that Mike had forgotten about medical school, but was too afraid to ask.

They did the chores that day; had a dip in the creek, clothing optional and both lay in the sun on a blanket after managing nautical sex. As night fell Rachel fell asleep happy; it was two days in a row.

Quite a Day

After finishing evening chores Rachel decided to head to the old restaurant where her and Gramps used to hang out. She sat on the patio at her old table, just staring at nothing when Gus arrived.

"Hey Rach how you doing?" If she was home she could just grab a beer, here a little trickier. Tonight she at least wanted to sit around people. The day had not gone well.

"Gus any way you can put some beer in a paper cup?"

"You ok?" She sighed,

"Be better with a beer." Gus could see it; she was generally a charming, upbeat sweetheart.

"Bad day?" She nodded,

"You could say that." Now Gus wasn't one of those nosey bartenders that played psychiatrist. But he had noticed that Rachel was alone; he had met her farmhand/boyfriend who now appeared to be missing. He detected something was afoot.

"I'll see what I can do." He came back in a second and set it down, gave her a wink.

"Anything to eat?" She looked distracted but gave him a little smile.

"I'll chew on this for awhile."

Meanwhile at the cottage next to the bar Marcus and Marie had settled down on the back deck to look at the river and sip Marie's favourite wine. She had met him at the airport; as usual he always came prepared with a few bottles of her favourite. Marcus had been taking in the scenery since he arrived. He didn't want to sound too enthusiastic but he really like what he saw. Canada was a huge country and Alberta was so much more open than Europe.

"So this is your old stomping ground?"

"Yep, the old hick town herself." Marcus got up and looked over the valley where the High River ran. Off in the distance was the Rocky Mountains, miles and miles of open land.

"It's quite pretty." Marie continued to not be impressed. He glanced over at the bar next to their cottage.

"Marie, unless I'm mistaken, your daughter is sitting at one of the tables."

"What!" Sure enough it was her all right. Hard to miss a copy of yourself and there was good old Rumble Doll, still running. She was shaking slightly and Marcus came up behind her and rubbed his hands up and down her arms. Marie was just staring, almost in disbelief, as I think you would if you saw a duplicate of yourself, that you created. She sniffed,

"The last time I saw her she was," she held out her hands, "this long." Now, look at her, she's." Marcus filled in the words.

"A beautiful young woman." She leaned against him; he whispered,

"What do you want to do?"

"I don't know." He reminded her.

"You came to meet her didn't you?"

"That was sort of the plan, but I can't just march up and say hi, it's mom." Now Marcus had mediated many labour negotiations, and was good at getting people with different opinions to be civil to each other. This would be another story.

"Let me go and talk to her, break the ice." She leaned back against him a little closer, so he could smell her hair.

"Would you?" Although it was not really a question.

So it was good old Marcus, looking after her again. He wandered over while Marie watched from the deck, sitting back with her sunglasses on in the shade of the porch overhang. The closer he got the more amazed he was at how much they looked alike. He stopped at respectful distance.

"Miss." She looked up from her beer, hoping it wasn't a cop. Gus would be in trouble.

"Yes."

"You're Rachel Bartlet right?"

"Yeah, who wants to know?" She wasn't feeling particularly friendly at the moment.

My name is Marcus Rossi." Even he was a little nervous at what her reaction would be. Her early body language was not good. She was waiting.

"Ok." He figured he'd just come out and say it.

"Long story short, I'm a friend of your mother's" She yelled out back into the bar.

"Gus, going to need another beer, now!" After that she was, surprisingly cool. Maybe she was getting used to things happening.

"Well pull up a seat Mr. Rossi; this is a story I got to hear." She took a long slug of her beer. Marcus noticed she was not doing well.

"Are you ok?" She laughed slightly.

"Oh, it's been quite a day, and now, this." She drained her beer and put down the empty cup firmly.

"Ok, kicked the crap out of that one!" Marcus leaned a little closer.

"You should know your mother wanted to know if you were ok, especially after we found out your Grandfather died." She was digesting the information and a good question occurred to her.

"How did you find that out?" Gus arrived with another cup of beer. He was also scoping out her new drinking partner and had never seen him before. Gus suspected he was looking to buy her a drink or something else.

"You ok darlin'?"

"I don't know yet." And remembering her western hospitality asked. "Mr. Rossi you want something?" He smiled at her and instantly liked her and felt a sorry she was in this position.

"Yes, something from the bar is definitely in order. Do you have any Scotch?" Gus nodded, still suspicious. He'd known Rachel for years and his immediate reaction was to be protective, but he was civil.

"You look like a single malt man, how's Glenlivet 14 year old?" Marcus was impressed, that he knew was not bar Scotch.

"Sounds good, give the bill to me for our drinks." Rachel held up her drink.

"Thanks Mr Rossi, I generally don't drink beer but Gus leads young girls astray." Gus stood smiling. He knew she was not having a great day but still had her sense of humour.

"Will that be all miss, or do you want to wait for another bus to throw me under?"

"No that's all, you're dismissed." Gus turned to Mr. Rossi."

"She takes liberties." She grinned and took a sip from her new cup.

"But I'm cute." She looked at the cup. "This stuff grows on you." Marcus could see Gus was getting concerned, and figured he should clear the air with him.

"Sir, I'm a friend of her mother's. I'll make sure the young lady gets home safely." Marie rolled her eyes as only a teenage girl can.

"So you going to be my new chauffeur?" She took a big gulp.

"Gus you should bring me another in case this one gets warm." Gus leaned in.

"Sweetheart I'm going to cut you off here." And gave her a little look. Rachel just shrugged, again only in a way that a teenage girl can. Now it was now back to business. Gus left, satisfied that she was in protective hands, but did wonder where the long lost mom was. She had never come up in conversation but obviously existed, somewhere.

"Ok, Marcus, where is good old mom?" Marcus sipped his whiskey. Rachel asked,

"Can I have some?" He smiled, being substitute fatherly.

"No." He could see the beer was starting to take effect. She stuck her tongue out at him and then remembered what they were talking about.

"Ok, what about good old mom?"

"She's waiting nearby to see if you want to see her; she's a little nervous." Rachel blurted out.

"No shit." Then she dropped the tough, smart girl routine, and sat back in her chair.

"I've had quite a day already." Marcus wondered what and had to ask.

"Something else!"

"Yeah, my farmhand took off today, left me a note." Marcus was getting clear signals that the farmhand was a little more than that.

"So, you're alone out there?" The beer had really kicked in and Rachel did have a filter problem.

"Yep, gave him everything and turns out he's just another horny guy on the road." Marcus could see the emotional pain on her young face, felt like going over and giving her a hug. But he'd known her ten minutes.

"Sorry, so maybe do the mom thing another day?" Just then Gus appeared just checking again things were ok with Rachel. Marcus gave him a little thumbs up. Rachel had decided.

"Let's do it all." Marcus took out his phone and texted her a message. Soon Rachel could see her coming, slowly. The closer she got the more obvious it became. It could have been a duplicate of herself. Her filter was completely useless now.

"Jesus mother of fuck!" Marie came and sat down next to Marcus.

"Hi Rachel." Rachel took a long look. It was almost like seeing a ghost. She said the word she never thought she would ever get to say.

"Mom?" Now all of us would think, what do you say after sixteen years? Both daughter and mother could come up with nothing. Nowhere in town was there a more awkward silence. Finally Marcus figured the situation needed a plan other than sit and stare at each other.

"Rachel is there room at the house for Marie and I?" She snapped out of it, but still staring at her mother while she talked.

"Sure, either in the bunkie or in the main house."

"Why don't I drive you home, Marie, bring your car and you two can have a sit and maybe think of something to say to each other." He did have a little tone in his voice. Both women gave him a look still wondering what to say, but truly had no idea. Rachel tossed him the keys and thought of something extremely rude to say but held it in.

"Ok Marcus, you drive a stick?" He nodded.

"Yes I can." The ride home was quiet as Rachel continued to wonder where all this was going, and was fighting off falling asleep. She was also a little plastered with two beer on an empty stomach. Marcus did keep glancing in the mirror to make sure Marie was still following. His doubts about her ability to carry this through was starting to enter his thoughts. The business man in him did wonder if Rachel could manage the farm on her own.

"Can you keep your place going by yourself?" She shrugged,

"Looks like I'm going to have to, think I'll stay clear of live in farmhands for awhile."

She had been thinking about it all and knew Mike was on a road trip, and landed with her by accident. To expect him to stay permanently was her being overly romantic. One question finally occurred to her.

"How long you known mom?"

"About a year."

"So you're a thing?"

"Oh yes we are a thing. This is a nice old car by the way." Rachel smiled.

"You know its back story?" Marcus nodded.

"Some I think." Rachel pointed to the driveway.

"Well we're here." On the drive down the lane Marcus was impressed. The place was neat and organized, quite a few cows grazing in the pasture next to the barn. Like most farms you got no idea from looking at it how much work it takes to maintain what looks like a gentle pastoral picture.

Well soon the new threesome were sitting on the deck of the Bartlet place. Many things came back to Marie as she sat and looked around, none of them positive. Listening to

Bible discussions on the back deck, farm chores. Cows peeing on her like a waterfall if you got too close. All the resentment and none of the good thoughts came back.

Marcus noticed the same problem that was at the bar was here. Neither of them could come up with where to start. It did occur to him that Rachel was the child in this relationship and it was up the her mother to make an effort to make amends as Rachel really did nothing wrong. It didn't appear to be happening, so finally he said,

"I have an idea." Both women looked at him, both in some ways glad he filled the silence with something.

"I like it here and am willing to help Rachel with the work that needs to be done. I am anything but a farmer but I assume most of it can be taught. Marie and I can stay in the bunkie and maybe Marie could pitch in where she can." He turned and looked at Marie. "I think Rachel needs a break, I don't know anything about farming but this is a big operation to work alone. I am not prepared to leave until she says she's ok. How's that sound like a plan?" Rachel was first,

"Sounds good, thank you, I could use a hand, but I'm going to fall asleep in my chair. I'll say my goodnights." Marie could only muster,

"Good night Rachel." When she had gone Marcus asked,

"Are you ok with all this?" She nodded.

"Yes, let's see how tomorrow goes. I'm tired Marcus, going to sleep." He nodded.

"I'm going to look at the stars, maybe have a little Scotch, brought my own." She leaned over and kissed him and left. Marcus had questions but thought, let's not ruin a beautiful night with the truth.

He sat and pondered his future and had maybe a few too many scotches. He was completely ready to change his lifestyle and location. He leaned back and actually took the time to notice the sky, actually, any sky. There had to be a trillion stars, never seen that many before, too much backlighting around European cities. Then the comet show started, never seen that either but knew what they were. He was not currently sharing Marie's view of High River. He found the place beautiful and was developing a growing protective feeling towards what he still viewed in his mind, a little girl.

Breakfast

Marcus woke up fairly early and looked over and discovered what he suspected would happen but didn't want to believe it. She was gone; he knew he didn't have to do a search. Marie was seldom ready to receive before noon. He got up and looked out, just for the heck of it.

" No car." Now he thought about calling her but knew there was no point. She'd run away from her daughter, again, and this time, him as well. He had a flare of anger, wondering how she could just run off and leave. Him, well, he almost got, but to leave her lovely daughter again, was unconscionable.

"Well nothing to do but make coffee." He wandered out into the kitchen perhaps looking for a note, not that they help much. He decided right then that even if she gets in touch with him down the road; they were done.

Though he never had any kids of his own he couldn't believe she would walk away from Rachel after meeting her. He sat on the porch admiring the mountains in the background and just sipped coffee. Her heard a noise and it was sleepy Rachel in her p.j.s. She wandered out and flopped down in a chair with a coffee. Always up early for chores and today was no different from any other. She did look a little like an unmade bed. He asked,

"How you feeling?" She rolled her head towards him,

"Little dry, I'll be fine; mom still sleeping?" He put his coffee down and sat up. She knew something was up and there was no good way to say this but,

"She's gone Rachel." She took a sip of her coffee.

"Did we get a note? Got a note from the last one."

"No, no note." She sort of laughed,

"Well they don't help much anyway." Then she lost it; this was the third strike, her Gramps dying, Mike leaving and now good old mom, resurrected from the past, but obviously her daughter was not worthy of any of her time.

She got up and went to Marcus and sat in his lap and cried on his chest till his shirt was wet. He held her little shaking sobbing body and felt so sorry for her. It was all he could do though was close to a total stranger but she just needed someone to give a shit. He just held her until she finally slowed down. You can only cry so long. Her Gramps had said a few times.

"Don't matter how we feel or what we're going through, the animals have to be fed, watered and cared for." She looked at him with red eyes,

"I got to do chores." Marcus thought, may as well tell her right now.

"Rachel this is what I was going to say to the three of us, but now it's two. I like this place; and I like you. I've spent my adult life behind a desk and I want a change. I was hoping your mother did as well, but I guess not. I'll stay in the bunkie and help you do chores and you can teach me what I need to know. I know I'm pretty close to a stranger but I want to help. I'm not leaving unless you tell me to. And there are no strings of any kind." He smiled. "Also on the only bright side, I've got lots of money, what you need around here I got it covered." He paused, " If you want to out and move on. I can help with that. Your place is worth about 3.5 million Canadian dollars with the milk quota. What do you think you want me to do?" She wiped the tears away.

"You know this place is 365, year round. But, I don't want to sell, it's my home." She almost laughed wiping more tears off her face. "So you want to be a farmer, why would you want to do that?"

"I do, and, I ain't leaving till you tell me. I'll be honest, never had a daughter, and I'm not suggesting I'm a dad substitute for you. I just like you and if there was ever a kid around who needed a break, it's you."

So he stayed, Marcus the business man became Marcus the farmer. At the end of the day they both sat, dog tired sipping beer looking out and the fields. One day he looked over and said,

"Rachel, does this ever seem weird to you?" She thought,

"Heck yeah. You know my friend Marcie who dropped by?" Marcus nodded.

"She thinks you're hot, wants to know if I'll share you." Marcus was actually shocked.

"What did you tell her." She leaned closer and whispered.

"I said, no way; we're getting married next week." Marcus knew she was kidding and laughed. The lovely little girl had not lost her sense of humour through all this.

"Gus was right, you take liberties." Then Rachel got serious.

"I tell anyone who asks, you're are my guardian angel, and I'm so glad you're here." She took a sip of her beer.

"Here's a question though, you ever look at me and see good old mom?" He took a sip of his whiskey.

"I thought that might be the hard part; but honestly when I look at you I don't see her, I see a little girl I just want to look out for. I know you're not a little girl, but that's how I see you. Maybe you are a daughter substitute. Now I do have a couple of suggestions." She jumped up,

"Another whiskey?" He laughed,

"Leading me astray?" She headed for the kitchen to get beer, calling back.

"That's funny." She came back with more beer, and a whiskey.

"Here's your liquid fire. So what's the suggestions?"

"I think you need some time to be a kid. How about I round up a couple of farm hands, give you the weekend off. I don't know, go skiing in the winter, flirt, whatever you want to do. I can take off Monday and Tuesday. I hear there's good skiing close by. What do you think?"

"Or, how about we both take the same weekend off and I'll ski with you." She leaned closer with her beer in her hand.

"But if you come back and there's a sock on the door, you'll have to bugger off." He smiled,

"What if you come back and I beat you getting the sock on the door?" She laughed,

"You'll never round up a snow bunny, you're too old." He took a look at her and shook his head. He felt so good she was comfortable enough to joke with him. Then he got a little serious.

"I have no idea how your mother could walk away from you." Rachel had thought about it a lot.

"From the stories Gramps told, I think mom hated this place and anything to do with it. Maybe she got broken somehow, losing her mother and sister. Or, maybe she's been thinking about herself so long she can't think about anyone else. And I think she just looked at me and just didn't care enough to stay." Marcus drained his glass.

"That's heavy thinking for a kid." She kicked her feet up on the railing and sipped her beer. "That's what I think." He looked at her with complete admiration; she was a lot tougher than she looked. Also, pretty intuitive for a sixteen year old She looked over,

"Your glass is empty again!" Marcus smiled.

"Evaporation." She grabbed it and got up to get his another one. When she came back she said,

"I'm cutting you off after this one. And, can I ask you a question?" He sipped his drink.

"Of course."

"I used to ask Gramps this but he only knew her as a young girl. What was she like with you?"

"Well, I can tell you what I saw, but I'm not sure she wasn't just acting. She was fun to be around, smart, well read, interested in boating and skiing, really fit." Rachel giggled,

"Good in the sack I bet." Marcus blushed and laughed,

"How can you say that and not blush?" Rachel shrugged.

"The blush got fucked out of me over the summer." His mouth dropped open and he actually choked on his whiskey.

"You are something, you know that?" She shrugged again,

"And I'm cute, so no comments on how my good old mom was?"

"Can't say kid, gentlemen don't kiss and tell." Rachel nodded.

"My Gramps used to say that." Rachel held up her beer.

"Going to change the farm name to Bartlet and Rossi."

So the new blended family sat and talked about a life they didn't completely understand. All Marcus knew was he was not leaving this little girl, and Rachel was so glad to have someone in her corner again. As far as we know they are still together, looking after the farm, but they would be stories for another time.

Dear reader,

Hope you enjoyed my slightly raunchy story. Don't really know much about farming but spent a fair amount of time on one as a kid. They were good times and remembered fondly. As usual if you have any questions about this story or any others you can contact me via email or look up my website. It is the opening info page.

Best wishes and good sailing

Made in the USA
Middletown, DE
20 May 2021